Nico

Visits the Moon

Written & Illustrated by Honorio Robledo

N ico woke up from his nap and crawled out of bed. Well, it wasn't really a bed. It was just a mattress on the floor because Nico was always tossing and turning at night and falling out of bed. The mattress on the floor solved that problem. The bedroom door was open. Nico crawled out into the hallway.

N ico crawled past the living room. Mommy was busy trying out some new nail polish. The tips of her fingers glowed like a neon sign. Daddy didn't see him because he was glued to the TV, watching the most important basketball game in the whole world.

There were balloons everywhere. Nico's mother and father had hung almost everything from balloons so Nico couldn't touch things. They did this because when Nico touched things he always got into trouble.

Like the time Nico touched a jar of honey. The house filled up with flies, who love sticky honey. So Nico's mother let an army of ants march across the kitchen floor to clean up the honey. But the house filled up with so many ants that Nico's father had to hire a herd of anteaters from Australia. The anteaters ate all the ants, but they were covered with fleas and the fleas jumped off the anteaters. Soon the whole house was full of fleas. Nico's mother and father said the fleas were all Nico's fault. That's why he was in trouble. And that's why they hung everything from balloons.

But let's not lose track of our story…

Nico crawled past the living room and…WOW! What a surprise! Somebody had left the front door open. A cool breeze drifted in from outside, carrying the delicious aromas of neighborhood kitchens and flower gardens. Nico poked his head out onto the porch. His friends the kittens—"Fast Claws" and "Mr. Tongue"—had already escaped and were playing on the stairs and the lawn.

And the balloons were slipping out the door and filling the sky with colors. So many balloons were in the sky it looked like a birthday party! Or maybe a carnival!

How sad! Nico couldn't join the celebration because the safety gate was locked. So he grabbed a balloon, and then another, and then another. He began to float up into the sky. That's when Mommy saw him and shrieked, "Nico, my goodness! Nico!" But it was too late. Nico was rising rapidly above the neighborhood. Soon he was higher than the antennas on the highest buildings. He looked like a little comet. In the distance he could see the ocean. It was an endless metallic blue.

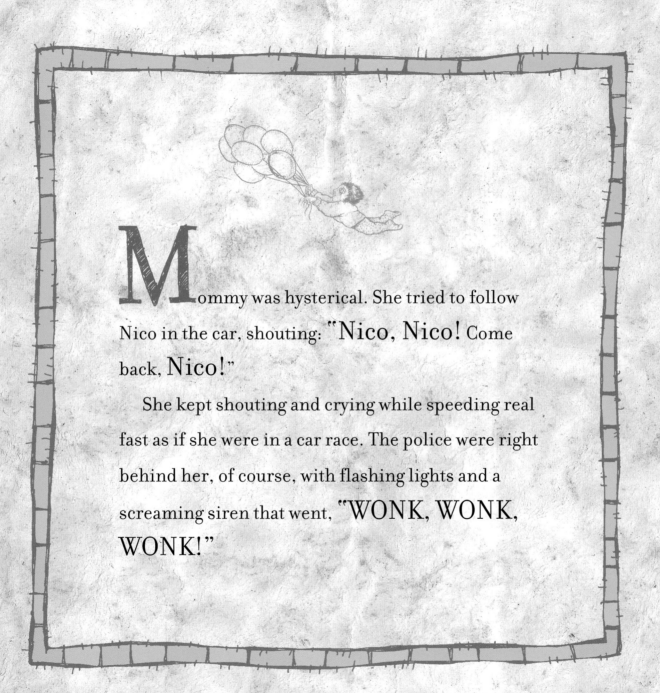

Mommy was hysterical. She tried to follow Nico in the car, shouting: "Nico, Nico! Come back, Nico!"

She kept shouting and crying while speeding real fast as if she were in a car race. The police were right behind her, of course, with flashing lights and a screaming siren that went, "WONK, WONK, WONK!"

Daddy tried to follow his little Nico, too. He turned off the most important basketball game in the world, and he gathered all of the leftover balloons in his hands, but he couldn't get off the ground. Not even an inch. He was too big! He was too old!

The firemen and the police couldn't catch him either. But they didn't have the right kind of equipment for rescuing little boys who were floating into the sky on balloons. In fact, nobody has the right kind of equipment for that.

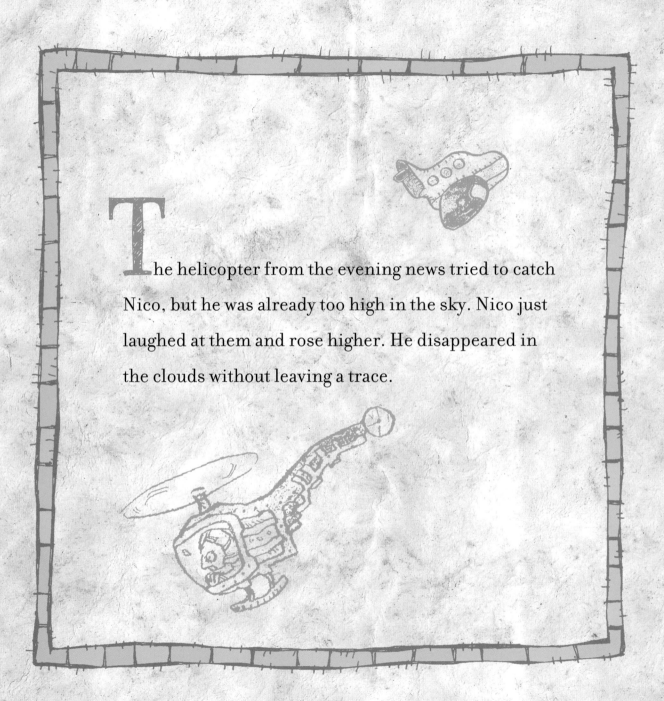

The helicopter from the evening news tried to catch Nico, but he was already too high in the sky. Nico just laughed at them and rose higher. He disappeared in the clouds without leaving a trace.

That night, on every television set in the whole city, people watched as Nico floated in and out of the clouds. They were astounded at what they saw! Nico was giggling and taking bites out of the soft clouds—like they were cotton candy! And he was playing tunes on the clouds—like they were bongo drums!

Nico's mother and father watched the news too. Mommy couldn't stop biting her nails, even though she had spent all that time painting them to look like neon signs. And Daddy was so sad he didn't even care who won the most important basketball game in the world.

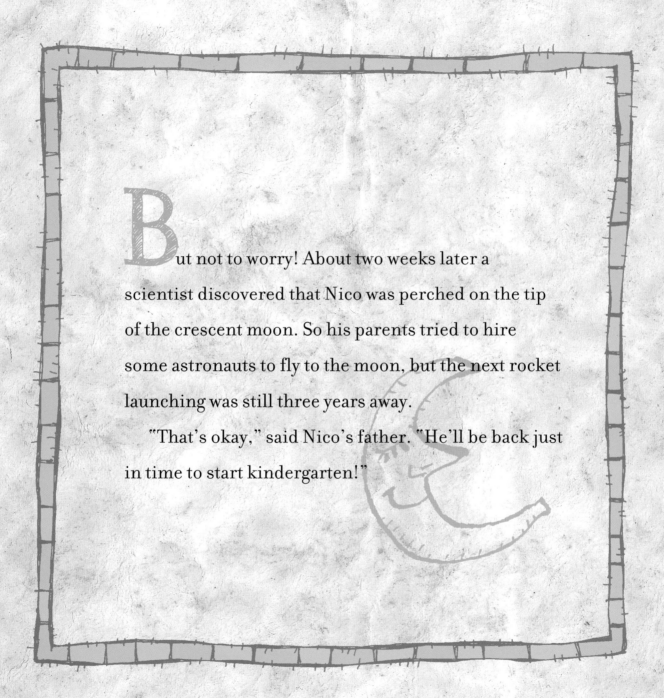

But not to worry! About two weeks later a scientist discovered that Nico was perched on the tip of the crescent moon. So his parents tried to hire some astronauts to fly to the moon, but the next rocket launching was still three years away.

"That's okay," said Nico's father. "He'll be back just in time to start kindergarten!"

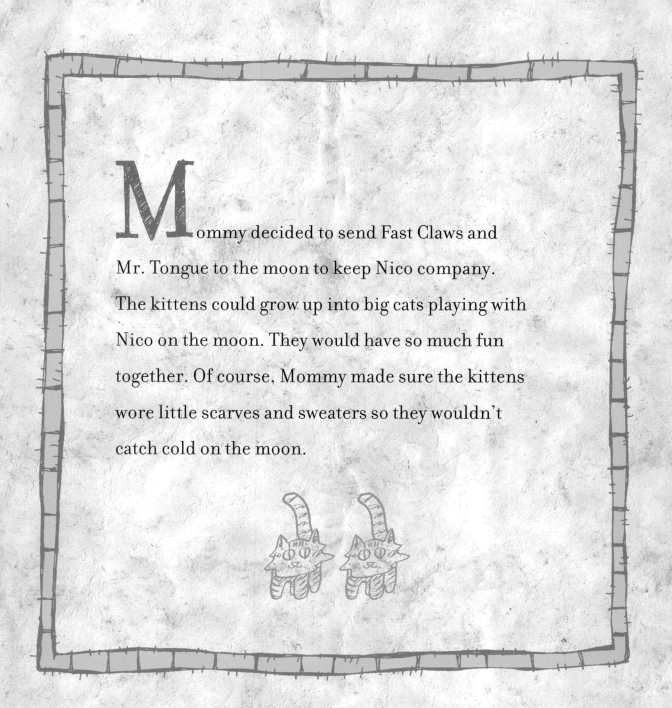

Mommy decided to send Fast Claws and Mr. Tongue to the moon to keep Nico company. The kittens could grow up into big cats playing with Nico on the moon. They would have so much fun together. Of course, Mommy made sure the kittens wore little scarves and sweaters so they wouldn't catch cold on the moon.

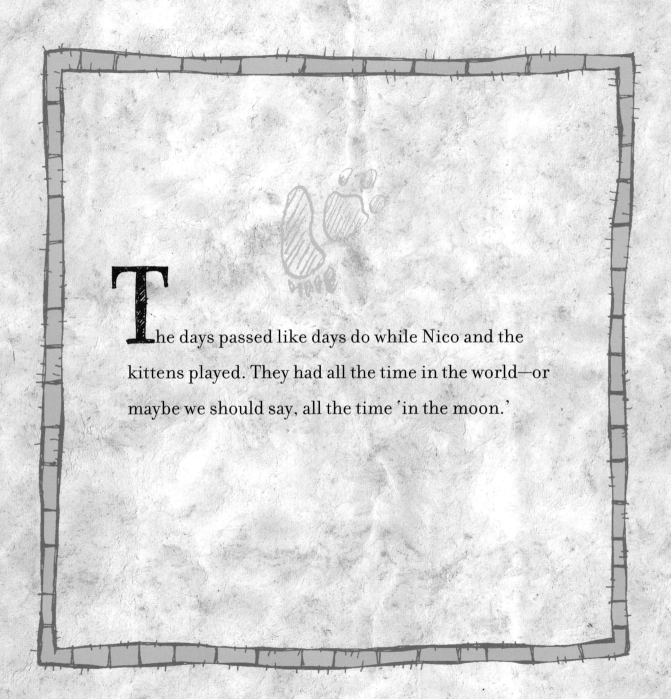

The days passed like days do while Nico and the kittens played. They had all the time in the world—or maybe we should say, all the time 'in the moon.'

And every day, Nico's mother sent hot chocolate and cookies and hamburgers and French fries and Daddy's special fried fish whenever he made it. Of course, her packages of food were usually cold when they reached the moon. And sometimes they never made it all the way to the moon because there were many strange creatures who grabbed the packages so they could eat up all the food.

Nico's mother and father always sent lots of love too, but the strange creatures never grabbed the packages of love because love was something they couldn't eat. So Nico always got plenty of love.

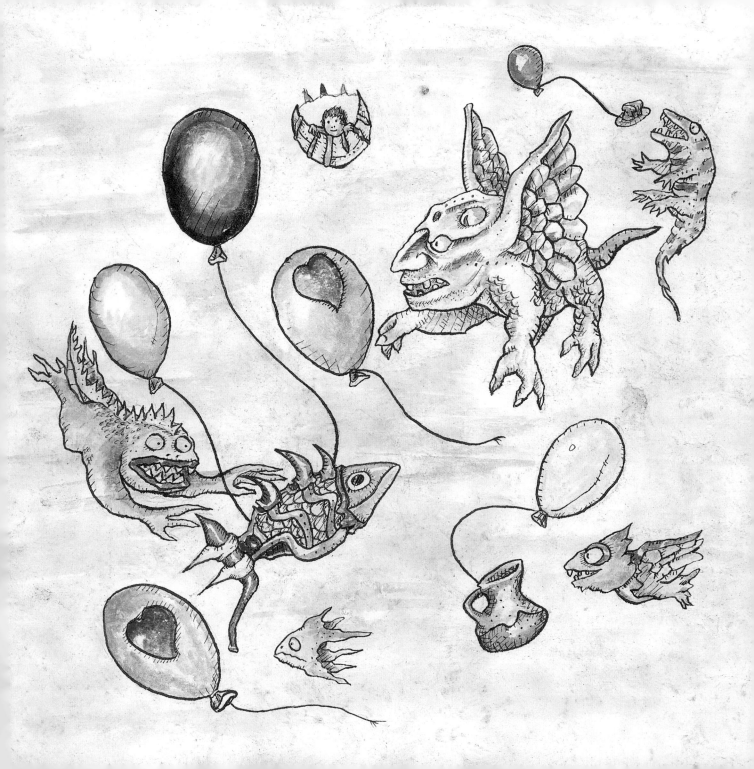

But Nico never worried about food. That's because on the moon there's less gravity to hold him to the ground, so Nico didn't get hungry very often. Neither did the kittens. When Nico got too much food from his mother, he just leaned over the edge of the moon and dropped it back to the earth. So if something yummy comes dropping through your window—like hot chocolate or cookies or burritos or French fries or fried fish—you'll know who to thank.

By the way, Nico's father was right. Three years after Nico floated to the moon, the astronauts went to pick him up. And he came back home with those big fat cats, Fast Claws and Mr. Tongue, just in time to start kindergarten.

Printed in Hong Kong by Morris Printing.

First Edition

10 9 8 7 6 5 4 3 2 1

Library of Congress Cataloging-in-Publication Data

Robledo, Honorio.
    [Nico visits the moon. Spanish]
    Nico visita la luna / escrito e ilustrado por Honorio Robledo.-- 1. ed.
       p. cm.
    ISBN 0938317-57-1
    [1. Moon--Fiction. 2. Cats--Fiction.]   I. Title.
    PZ73 .R575 2001
    [E]--dc21

2001028079

To Luana, my wife.
To Nicolás, to Amalia, my children. H.R.

Book and cover design by Antonio Castro H.